Teachers, librarians, and kids from across Canada are talking about the *Canadian Flyer Adventures*. Here's what some of them had to say:

Great Canadian historical content, excellent illustrations, and superb closing historical facts (I love the kids' commentary!). ~ SARA S., TEACHER, ONTARIO

As a teacher–librarian I welcome this series with open arms. It fills the gap for Canadian historical adventures at an early reading level! There's fast action, interesting, believable characters, and great historical information. ~ MARGARET L., TEACHER–LIBRARIAN, BRITISH COLUMBIA

The *Canadian Flyer Adventures* will transport young readers to different eras of our past with their appealing topics. Thank goodness there are more artifacts in that old dresser ... they are sure to lead to even more escapades. ~ SALLY B., TEACHER–LIBRARIAN, MANITOBA

When I shared the book with a grade 1–2 teacher at my school, she enjoyed the book, noting that her students would find it appealing because of the action-adventure and short chapters. ~ HEATHER J., TEACHER AND LIBRARIAN, NOVA SCOTIA

Newly independent readers will fly through each *Canadian Flyer Adventure*, and be asking for the next installment! Children will enjoy the fast-paced narrative, the personalities of the main characters, and the drama of the dangerous situations the children find themselves in. ~ PAM L., LIBRARIAN, ONTARIO

I love the fact that these are Canadian adventures—kids should know how exciting Canadian history is. Emily and Matt are regular kids, full of curiosity, and I can see readers relating to them. ~ JEAN K., TEACHER, ONTARIO

What kids told us:

I would like to have the chance to ride on a magical sled and have adventures. ~ EMMANUEL

I would like to tell the author that her book is amazing, incredible, awesome, and a million times better than any book I've read. ~ MARIA

I would recommend the *Canadian Flyer Adventures* series to other kids so they could learn about Canada too. The book is just the right length and hard to put down. ~ PAUL

The books I usually read are the full-of-fact encyclopedias. This book is full of interesting ideas that simply grab me. ~ ELEANOR

At the end of the book Matt and Emily say they are going on another adventure. I'm very interested in where they are going next! ~ ALEX

I like when Emily and Matt fly into the sky on a sled towards a new adventure. I can't wait for the next book! ~ JI SANG

Yikes, Vikings!

Frieda Wishinsky

Illustrated by Dean Griffiths

MAPLE
TREE
PRESS

Maple Tree Press Inc.
51 Front Street East, Suite 200, Toronto, Ontario M5E 1B3
www.mapletreepress.com

Text © 2007 Frieda Wishinsky   Illustrations © 2007 Dean Griffiths

Distributed in Canada by Raincoast Books
9050 Shaughnessy Street, Vancouver, British Columbia V6P 6E5

Distributed in the United States by Publishers Group West
1700 Fourth Street, Berkeley, California 94710

Dedication
For my friends Mira and Arlene Coviensky

Acknowledgements
Many thanks to the hard-working Maple Tree team—Sheba Meland, Anne Shone, Grenfell
Featherstone, Deborah Bjorgan, Cali Hoffman, Dawn Todd, and Erin Walker—for their insightful
comments and steadfast support. Special thanks to Dean Griffiths and Claudia Dávila for their
engaging and energetic illustrations and design.

Cataloguing in Publication Data
Wishinsky, Frieda
Yikes, vikings! / Frieda Wishinsky ; illustrated by Dean Griffiths.

(Canadian flyer adventures ; 4)
ISBN-13: 978-1-897066-96-6 (bound) / ISBN-10: 1-897066-96-1 (bound)
ISBN-13: 978-1-897066-97-3 (pbk.) / ISBN-10: 1-897066-97-X (pbk.)

1. Leiv Eiriksson, d. ca. 1020—Juvenile fiction. 2. Vikings—Juvenile fiction.
I. Griffiths, Dean, 1967– II. Title. III. Series: Wishinsky, Frieda. Canadian flyer adventures ; 4.

PS8595.I834Y55 2007   jC813'.54   C2007-901861-0

Design & art direction: Claudia Dávila
Illustrations: Dean Griffiths

We acknowledge the financial support of the Canada Council   ONTARIO ARTS COUNCIL
for the Arts, the Ontario Arts Council, the Government   CONSEIL DES ARTS DE L'ONTARIO
of Canada through the Book Publishing Industry Development Program (BPIDP), and the
Government of Ontario through the Ontario Media Development Corporation's Book Initiative
for our publishing activities.

Printed in Canada
Ancient Forest Friendly: Printed on 100% Post-Consumer Recycled Paper

A   B   C   D   E   F

CONTENTS

HOW IT ALL BEGAN

Emily and Matt couldn't believe their luck. They discovered an old dresser full of strange objects in the tower of Emily's house. They also found a note from Emily's Great-Aunt Miranda: "The sled is yours. Fly it to wonderful adventures."

They found a sled right behind the dresser! When they sat on it, shimmery gold words appeared:

Rub the leaf
Three times fast.
Soon you'll fly
To the past.

The sled rose over Emily's house. It flew over their town of Glenwood. It sailed out of a cloud and into the past. Their adventures on the flying sled had begun! Where will the sled take them next? Turn the page to find out.

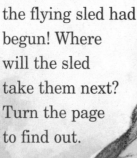

Viking, Vinland
1001

1

Knock

Knock! Knock!

Emily opened her eyes. She glanced at her clock. It was nine. Her mom hated it when she slept late, even on Saturday.

Knock! Knock!

"I'll be up soon, Mom!" she called.

"It's not your mom," answered Matt from the other side of the door. "Come on, Em. Get up."

"Go away. It's too early." Emily turned over and pulled the quilt over her head.

"But I know where we should go on our next adventure. It'll be awesome!"

"I haven't brushed my teeth. I haven't combed my hair. I'm not even out of bed," grumbled Emily.

"I'll wait downstairs until you're ready," replied Matt. "Your mom just baked blueberry muffins. She said I could have some."

Emily sighed. It was no use trying to sleep. She was wide-awake now. She kicked off the covers and sat up. Mmmm. Those muffins smelled sweet and buttery.

Emily slid out of bed. She brushed her teeth and hair, and slipped into her jeans and red T-shirt. Then she ran down to join Matt in the kitchen.

"Hi, Em," he mumbled, his mouth full of muffin. His lips were blue. "These are great. I've had three already."

"Where's my mom?" asked Emily. She helped herself to a muffin and a glass of milk.

"She's in the backyard."

Emily sat across from Matt at the kitchen table. "So where do you want to go?" she asked.

"To meet Leif Eriksson in Vinland," said Matt. "I saw an old cap labeled *Viking, Vinland, 1001* in the dresser before our last adventure. And Eric Swenson, who's in my class, told us that Leif and the Vikings were the first Europeans to discover North America—even before Columbus."

Emily's eyes lit up. "I love Vikings. They sailed on ships with scary dragons carved in front, and they wore big, pointy helmets with horns."

Emily grabbed a paper napkin and drew a tall Viking on a ship.

"Eric said Vikings never wore helmets with horns."

"He doesn't know that for sure," said Emily. "He didn't go to Viking times. But we can. And if Vikings wore those crazy helmets, I'm going to try one on!"

2

Into the Woods

Matt led the way up the rickety stairs to the tower. As soon as he pushed the door open, he rushed over to the dresser and opened the top drawer.

"Here it is!" Matt showed Emily the old cap with the label.

"So, what are we waiting for?" said Emily. "Let's go sailing!"

Matt saluted. "Aye aye, sir!"

Matt slipped the cap back in the drawer. He and Emily hopped on the sled.

Immediately,   shimmery   gold   words

appeared around the maple leaf painted on the front of the *Canadian Flyer*.

Rub the leaf
Three times fast.
Soon you'll fly
To the past.

Matt rubbed the leaf and a thick fog enveloped them. When it lifted, they were flying!

"Look at our clothes," said Matt as they sailed out of a cloud. "We look like Vikings already!" They each wore a belted tunic top, loose pants, leather shoes that looked like slippers, and a cap like the one they'd found in the dresser.

"But we don't have any helmets with horns yet," said Emily. "I have my sketchbook, though." She patted a leather pouch at her waist.

6

"My digital recorder's here, too," said Matt, peeking inside his pouch.

The sled flew down toward a long, sandy beach surrounded by woods. "That must be Vinland!" shouted Matt. "But where are the Vikings and their ship?"

"Maybe they're exploring nearby," said Emily as they landed.

Emily and Matt stood up and looked around. Waves rolled toward the shore. Seagulls squawked overhead. But there were no people anywhere.

"Let's look in the woods," suggested Matt. "We can leave the sled behind this big rock."

Emily shivered. "Those woods are dark."

"We won't go far." Matt peered into the forest. "There might be a clearing where the Vikings built houses. Or they might be hunting for food."

"Do they hunt with bows and arrows?" asked Emily.

"Yes. And spears," said Matt.

"Let's talk loudly so they don't accidentally hunt us."

They walked into the woods. "Hello!" called Matt.

"Don't shoot! We're kids!" called Emily.

Insects buzzed and birds chattered. But there were no people anywhere.

The deeper they walked into the forest, the closer the trees grew. The forest grew darker and darker. They could barely see.

Matt tripped on a tree root. "Ouch!" he cried.

"Are you all right?" asked Emily.

"I'm okay. But let's get out of here. These woods are creepy."

They ran out of the woods toward the sunlit beach.

"Yahoo! Sun!" sang Matt.

"But no Vikings."

Emily flopped down against a log on the beach beside the rock where they'd left the sled.

Matt sat beside her. He turned on his recorder. "This is Matt reporting from—I don't know where. All I know is that Emily and I are looking for Leif Eriksson and his Vikings in Vinland in 1001. But there are no Vikings here. Where are they? Where are we? What year is it?"

"What do we do now?" asked Emily.

"I don't know," said Matt, shutting his recorder off.

"Maybe the sled dumped us in the wrong place. Or maybe it's the wrong year. Maybe we should try to go home."

Matt sighed. "Let's wait a little longer."

Emily looked back at the woods. She looked out to sea. She saw no one. They were alone.

3

Discovered

"Who are you?"

Matt opened his eyes. Emily was still asleep. They'd both fallen asleep on the beach.

A tall, bearded man stood over them. Behind him stood four other men. They wore tunics, loose pants, cloaks fastened with silver brooches, caps, and leather shoes. A dagger hung from each man's belt.

Yikes! thought Matt. *They must be Vikings!* Matt glanced down at the beach. A little boat was pulled up on land. And a Viking ship bobbed up and down in the bay.

"Wake up, Emily." Matt nudged her. She opened her eyes and stared at the men.

"I am Leif Eriksson," said the tall man. "Answer me! Who are you and what are you doing here?"

Even though Leif Eriksson must have been speaking a Norse language, Matt could understand him. "I-I'm Matt. And this is Emily," he stammered. "W-we..." Now that the famous Viking was standing beside them, Matt's tongue felt as if it were glued to the roof of his mouth.

"Speak up," demanded Leif Eriksson. His eyes bored right through Matt, as if he could read his thoughts. "And what is that?" Leif pointed to the sled.

"It-it's—," Matt mumbled.

"It's a flying sled," Emily blurted out.

Matt stared at her in horror.

"Are you telling me that this piece of wood flies like a bird?" said Leif.

"Yes," said Emily. "We're from the future, and it's a magic sled. It flew us here."

"Emily," said Matt under his breath. "What are you saying?"

"I couldn't think of anything else," whispered Emily.

Matt waited for Leif Eriksson to yell at them and call them liars. But Leif's face crinkled into a big smile. He roared with laughter.

"This is the best tale I have heard since we left Greenland," he said. "Now, tell me the truth. I am sure your family heard Bjarni Herjolfsson's stories just as we did."

"We don't know anyone called Bjarni," said Emily.

"Nonsense!" boomed Leif. "How else would

14

you have known of this place? Bjarni told many people that he sighted new land when his ship blew off course."

"Is this Vinland?" asked Matt.

"This place has no name. We have just landed here. Where is your family?"

"Home," said Emily.

"I see," said Leif, stroking his beard. "Were you playing in the woods? Did their ship sail without you?"

"W-we..." Matt looked at Emily. She shrugged. She couldn't think of anything either.

"I see you are frightened. But what do I do with you now? This land has fine timber, but it is only the second place Bjarni described. We are sailing on to more fertile land. We are leaving *now*."

4

Who's Afraid of Dragons?

"Can we come with you?" asked Emily. "We can help on your ship."

"Help!" said Leif Eriksson laughing. "Can you fish? Cook? Clean?"

"I can fish," said Emily. It was sort of true. Emily had gone fishing twice, although all she'd caught was a bunch of weeds.

"I can cook," said Matt. It was almost true. He'd made scrambled eggs once, although they were so dry that no one ate them. But he'd tried.

"I see," said Leif.

"Our ship is crowded enough already," grunted one of the Vikings.

"Gunnar is right," said Leif, turning to the Viking behind him. Gunnar was as tall as Leif with shoulders as wide as a football player.

"We're not big," said Emily. "We don't take up much room."

Leif Eriksson laughed. "They speak the truth, Gunnar. They are not big, and they tell good tales. It would be cruel to leave them in this deserted place." He looked sternly at Emily and Matt. "If we take you with us, you will work. Understood?"

Matt and Emily nodded.

"And bring your flying wood," growled Gunnar, pointing to the sled. "It will be useful."

"Useful?" said Emily. "Why?"

Emily didn't like the way Gunnar was

eyeing the sled as if it belonged to him.

"Enough questions," grunted Gunnar as they piled into the small boat. They pushed off from shore.

"I bet the next place is Vinland," Matt whispered to Emily.

"Why do you whisper?" barked Gunnar. "What is this place called Vinland?"

Matt cleared his throat. He couldn't explain that he knew about Vinland from the future.

"I-I heard there's a land close by that has vines full of grapes," he stammered.

"You children are full of stories," said Leif, laughing. "But grapes? I think not."

Emily and Matt gaped as they rowed closer and closer to the Viking ship. It was wider than they had imagined. It had a big square sail, a single mast, and a large steering oar in the stern. But no carved dragons.

"Where are the dragons?" Emily asked.

"This is a *knorr*, a trading ship," said Leif. "There are only dragons on warships. Are you frightened of dragons?"

"No," said Emily. "There are no such things."

"Are you sure?" asked Leif, raising his eyebrows. "Perhaps there are dragons in the next land. And if there are, are you brave enough to face them?"

"I've faced dinosaurs," said Emily. "Dragons can't be any scarier than a T. rex. You should have seen its teeth!"

"T. rex? Dinosaurs? I know nothing of such creatures," Leif said. "But we will soon see if you are brave. We will soon know if you are true Vikings."

A Gift from the Sea

"Hurry. Get on board," Gunnar ordered Emily and Matt. "We have no time to waste." Gunnar scowled at them as if they were smelly fish.

"Here." A grey-haired sailor, who stood on the deck of the Viking ship, held out his hand to help Emily aboard. "I am Tyrkir," he said as he hoisted Emily and the sled over the rail.

"I'm Emily. Thanks."

"Now you," said Gunnar, giving Matt a sharp shove. "Or are you too weak to climb in yourself?"

"I can manage," Matt muttered. He grabbed

the side of the rail and tried to yank himself up. But his hand slipped, and he fell back on top of Gunnar.

"You stupid oaf!" yelled the burly Viking.

"Sorry," said Matt.

"Get off my stomach," said Gunnar, "and out of my sight!"

Matt grabbed the side of the rail again. With all his might, he pulled himself up. He got one foot over the rail. But just as he lifted his other foot, a seagull pooped on his cap.

"Oh no!" he groaned.

"A gift from the sea," said Tyrkir, laughing.

Matt didn't laugh. Leif and the other Vikings stepped aboard while Matt rubbed his cap against the wet wood on the side of the ship. Some of the poop fell off, but his cap still felt slimy.

"Did you get it all?" asked Emily.

"Yes. But now my cap's so cold and wet that I can't wear it," said Matt.

"Enough talk!" grunted Gunnar. "You are lucky to be here at all." Gunnar glared at them and stomped away.

"Look!" Emily pointed to the thirty or more Vikings on the ship. "No one's wearing a helmet with horns."

"I told you. Eric said they didn't," said Matt.

"Maybe they will later," said Emily, "Maybe they wear helmets like that on special occasions."

Leif strode to the steering oar. "Onward!" he commanded. Vikings manned rows of oars. The *knorr* began to move.

"Come," said Tyrkir to Emily and Matt. "You will help me clean fish. We have just caught some."

Emily and Matt followed Tyrkir to the bow of the ship. A pile of glistening fish lay in a hold, just below the deck. Some of the fish were dead, but some still wriggled.

Tyrkir handed fish to Matt and Emily. Matt's stomach heaved. He didn't want to stick his hands into fish guts. The expression of disgust on Emily's face told him she didn't want to clean fish either.

"Watch me," said Tyrkir. He showed them how to slice into a fish, clean off its scales, scrape its insides and throw the unused parts to the seagulls. "Now you," he said, handing Emily and Matt sharp knives. "But take care. Do not slice off your fingers."

Emily and Matt took deep breaths as they worked. It was hard not to throw up. The rolling motion of the ship made their stomachs feel even worse.

"Remember how we couldn't wait to sail on a Viking ship?" Matt whispered to Emily. "I've changed my mind."

"If I clean one more fish, I'll barf," said Emily.

"Only ten more," said Tyrkir, hurrying over. He patted them both on the back.

"*Only* ten more?" groaned Matt.

"I can't," moaned Emily.

"You must," said Tyrkir. "It is your job. And we must hurry. We will anchor before dark and cook the fish on shore. It will be a great feast."

6

A Fish Feast

Emily and Matt took long, deep breaths and cleaned another fish. Then another and another. Despite their queasy stomachs, they managed to clean all the fish without getting sick. As they scraped the last one, Leif steered the *knorr* toward shore.

"We will stay here for the night. We sail again in the morning," he declared.

When the ship was close enough to shore, all the Vikings jumped overboard. They waded in the knee-deep water and hauled the *knorr* up to the beach. They tied the bowline securely to some trees in the forest and hurried to gather wood before dark. Then they lit a huge bonfire. As the sun set, Tyrkir tied long, thick sticks together and placed them tee-pee style over the fire. He tied the fish to the wood to cook them. Soon, the smell of cooking fish filled the cool, night air.

"There is nothing like fresh fish from the sea," said Leif, smacking his lips.

The Vikings nodded and reached for chunks of smoky fish. They licked their fingers, savouring every bite. Then they wiped their hands on their tunics.

"For you," said Tyrkir, handing Emily and Matt each a roasted fish.

"I'm not hungry," said Matt. He couldn't eat fish after cleaning all those guts.

"Me neither," said Emily.

"You must eat," said Tyrkir.

"You need strength to work. Eat," insisted Leif.

Matt and Emily each picked up a small piece of fish.

"Here goes," said Matt. He closed his eyes and dropped a tiny piece of fish into his mouth. Then he opened his eyes and smiled.

"Hey, Em. Try it. It's good," he said.

"I don't like fish," said Emily.

"Eat," said Leif.

Emily sighed. Then she slowly lifted a piece of fish to her mouth. She closed her eyes and swallowed. She took another piece of fish and swallowed. Then a third and a fourth.

"Well?" asked Matt.

"I like it!" said Emily.

"It's another gift from the sea," said Tyrkir.

"It's a better gift than seagull poop," said Matt.

The Vikings howled with laughter.

"Spoken like a true Viking," said Leif, patting Matt so hard on the back that he fell forward.

After they'd all had their fill of fish, the Vikings spread blankets on the beach and slept.

Matt and Emily tried to sleep, but the Vikings snored so loudly that it was hard.

"They sound like truck engines," said Emily.

"They sound like my grandfather. His snoring makes the house shake."

"I'm so tired," said Emily, yawning. "I wish I could fall asleep."

"If only I could plug my ears with something," said Matt. "Hey, Em, why don't we—?"

But Emily was so tired that she'd fallen asleep despite the noise. And soon, so did Matt.

Before they knew it, Tyrkir was shaking them awake.

It was late morning.

"Hurry. The tide is up. We are leaving now," he said.

Matt and Emily opened their eyes. Sure enough, the Vikings were heading to the *knorr*. They were ready to launch the ship back into the sea.

7

Vikings Never Complain

Emily and Matt scrambled out of their warm blankets. They grabbed the sled and raced to the ship.

"You are lucky," snarled Gunnar, wading knee-deep into the ocean. "Vikings do not wait for lazy children."

"We are *not* lazy!" protested Emily. "It was hard to fall asleep last night. You were all snoring."

"Mind your tongue," barked Gunnar. He pointed his finger at Matt and Emily. "A Viking can sleep anytime, anywhere. And a Viking never complains. Now, help us push the *knorr* off the sandbar or be gone!"

"Do not mind Gunnar," said Tyrkir. "He has no patience with children, even his own three."

"Gunnar's a dad?" Emily whispered to Matt as she stepped into the icy water. "Can you imagine being *his* kid?"

Matt shook his head. He couldn't talk. He was using all his energy to help push the *knorr*.

"One. Two. Heave!" shouted Leif.

Sweat poured down every face. Seawater drenched every pant leg. Seaweed dangled like spaghetti from every tunic as they launched the ship back into the sea.

For two more days, the ship hugged the coast as they sailed south. On the third morning,

Leif called, "Island ahead! Head for shore!"

A roar of excitement exploded from the Vikings.

"This *has* to be Vinland," Matt whispered to Emily.

"How will we know?" asked Emily. "There won't be any Welcome to Vinland signs."

"We'll know if we find grapes."

"If we do," said Emily, "I'm going to eat buckets. Then I'm going to squish some into juice."

"Into the water!" shouted Leif.

"Not again," moaned Matt and Emily. The Vikings plunged into the ocean.

"Come help pull the ship, children," said Tyrkir, when they neared the shore. "Before Gunnar sees that you are not working."

Emily and Matt climbed over the rail of the ship.

"This water is icy," said Matt, shivering. "If only we could drink some hot chocolate to warm up when we finish."

"There's no hot chocolate in Viking times," said Emily. "There's only water and fish!"

"Heave!" shouted Leif.

They pulled and pulled, and soon the ship was on the beach.

The Vikings hurried up the shore. The land was lush and green.

"We will never want for food in this land," said Leif, pointing to schools of salmon in a nearby river.

"The salmon are so big, we will have trouble bringing them to camp," said Gunnar. "That is...unless—" Gunnar glanced at the sled.

"Oh no! That's why Gunnar wants the sled. He wants to load it with dead fish!" Emily whispered to Matt. "Yuck!"

8

Just a Little Way In

"Hurry," said Leif, gazing around the new land. "We must ready our campsite before dark. Tomorrow we will build huts. I am certain now that this is the land Bjarni described. The soil is rich. The grass is good for grazing cattle, and there are many fish."

Emily and Matt helped gather wood for the fire.

"I'm sick of fish!" said Emily, picking up an armful of fallen twigs and branches. "All the Vikings eat is fish. I wish I had a bologna sandwich."

"I wish I had grilled cheese," said Matt.

"Or a hot fudge sundae with bananas and whipped cream," said Emily. "And—"

"Come, children. We will fill your sled with the wood," said Tyrkir.

Emily and Matt helped Tyrkir load the wood. As they did, Gunnar glanced at the sled again.

"Gunnar keeps looking at the sled," whispered Emily. "I bet he wants to take it away from us. Then he'll load tons of fish on it. He won't be careful. He could even break it."

"We have to hide it," said Matt.

Soon everyone gathered around the fire to eat wild berries, wild greens, and fish.

When they finished their meal, Leif stood up. "We will begin exploring tomorrow. We do not know this land, so only half of you will explore at a time, and never alone. The other half will stay in camp. We must not lose anyone. There may be wild beasts or worse lurking in the forest." Then he bid them all goodnight.

Emily and Matt grabbed the sled and headed for the spot where Tyrkir said they'd build their hut tomorrow. They looked around. "Phew! I don't see Gunnar," said Emily. "Let's hide the sled in that prickly bush over there."

"Good," said Matt. "Those thorns should keep him away."

"Ouch!" Emily yelped as they shoved the sled under the bush. "The thorns in this bush are as sharp as needles. My fingers are bleeding."

"My arm's cut up, too," said Matt. "Gunnar wouldn't dare go near this nasty bush."

For the next two days, half the Vikings built huts and half explored the woods. Matt and Emily helped Tyrkir build the small hut the three of them would share.

After the hut was finished, Tyrkir told Emily and Matt to pick berries.

"I wish we could explore the woods instead of picking berries all day," said Emily. "Let's ask Leif if we can."

But Leif refused.

"It is safer for children to stay at the camp-site," Leif told them.

"Just *once?*" begged Emily. "No one's seen any wild beasts or dragons in the forest."

"No," said Leif. "That is my order."

The next day, as the Vikings headed for the forest, Tyrkir told Matt and Emily to pick berries again.

"Berries—again!" Matt complained to Emily. "My hands are black and blue from berry juice."

"And we still don't know if this is Vinland. Maybe it was all a story. Maybe there isn't a Vinland. No one's seen a single grape around here yet."

"The only way we'll know if there are grapes is if we explore the woods ourselves and find some," said Matt.

Emily's eyes lit up. "Let's explore tomorrow.

We can sneak out first thing in the morning, before anyone is up."

The next morning, Emily woke up just before the sun rose. She checked to see if Tyrkir was awake. Phew! He'd already left the hut. *He's probably out gathering wood*, thought Emily.

Emily tapped Matt on the shoulder. "Come on, Matt. Get up before Tyrkir gets back and sees us."

"My arms ache from picking berries. Just give me five more minutes to sleep," muttered Matt, rolling over.

"OK. I'll be back in five minutes to get you."

Emily walked outside. The air was crisp and cool. A fog hung over the shore like a grey curtain. She sat on a log and sketched the Viking ship in the mist.

Emily stood up, but before she could go back inside, she heard footsteps in the grass behind the hut. She peeked around.

Gunnar was dragging the sled out of the bush! He must have seen them hide it or guessed it was there! And he wanted the sled so much, he didn't care that his arm was bleeding from the thorns.

Emily raced inside the hut. She shook Matt. "Wake up! Gunnar is stealing our sled! We have to stop him."

"Yikes!" cried Matt. He popped out of bed and hurried outside with Emily. "I don't see him. Which way did he go?"

"I think he went thataway," said Emily, pointing to the forest. "But I'm not sure."

9

Lost

Matt and Emily headed for the forest. The fog was beginning to lift, but it was still dark in the woods.

"How will we know how to get back to the campsite?" asked Emily.

Matt pulled his knife from the pouch at his waist. "With this." He carved the letter *M* for Matt and the number *1* into the bark of the trees they passed. "We can follow the numbers and my initials all the way back."

"I want to carve my initials, too," said Emily.

Matt handed her his knife. Emily carved *E2* into the next tree.

As she did, Matt pulled out his recorder. "Ladies and gentlemen," he began.

Before he could say anything else, Emily grabbed his arm. "Matt, turn that off. I hear something."

Matt flipped the recorder off. "What do you hear?" he asked.

"A crunching, clicking sound."

They stopped walking and listened.

"I don't hear anything," Matt squinted into the forest.

"Listen. I hear it again. It must be a person."

"It's not a person. It's an animal," said Matt. "Over there!" Matt pointed to a tree.

A large creature with antlers was chomping on leaves.

"Wow! It looks like a giant reindeer," said Emily.

"I bet it's a caribou," said Matt. "They're like reindeers. Come on. Let's keep going."

As they walked on, they took turns carving their initials into the trees.

The sun shone through the trees, warming their faces. They passed three white hares hopping around. They heard birds chirping and saw bushes thick with blueberries, but they didn't see Gunnar, their sled, or a single grape.

"Maybe we shouldn't go any farther. We're getting far from the campsite," said Emily. "Even if he's in the woods now, Gunnar will have to go back before dark."

"But the sled may be broken by then. Let's walk for another few minutes and look for him. Then we'll turn back."

The leaves crackled beneath their feet as they headed farther into the forest. Then they stopped. Someone was sitting on a log. His head was cupped in his hands.

"It's Tyrkir!" Matt hurried toward the Viking.

Tyrkir looked up. "Children!" he exclaimed. "I am so happy to see you. I have been here since last night. I slipped out of our hut to catch a hare for tonight's supper and lost my way. Are Leif and the others behind you?"

"No," said Matt. "We came alone. But don't worry. We carved our initials into the trees, and it will be easy to find our way back."

"I don't think we carved anything for a while," said Emily. "We've been so busy looking that we forgot."

"You're right. But the last tree I carved into couldn't be far away."

"Which way though? Left or right?" asked Emily.

Matt looked left. Then right. He gulped. "I don't know."

10

Bunny Hop

Matt and Emily sat on the log beside Tyrkir. The sun beat down on their heads. For a few minutes no one spoke.

Matt wiped his brow. "I'm so hot, I can't think." He took off his cap and placed it on the ground beside him.

As soon as he did, a large hare hopped over and grabbed Matt's cap.

"Drop it!" shouted Matt. But the hare scampered away with Matt's cap between its teeth. Matt jumped up and ran after it.

"Matt, forget about your cap," shouted Emily.

"You're going to get even more lost."

"Emily! Tyrkir! Hurry!" yelled Matt.

Emily and Tyrkir rushed toward Matt. He was standing in a small clearing and pointing.

"Oh!" cried Tyrkir. "I do not believe it! Those are grapevines!" Tyrkir's eyes gleamed. "We must tell Leif and the men. They will be overjoyed."

Then Tyrkir's face fell. "But what if we do not find our way back?" he said.

"Don't worry," said Matt. "That big rabbit not only led me to the grapevines, but he also found our way back. I can see *E6* on the tree over there," said Matt, pointing. "We were walking in circles."

Emily raced toward the tree. "Hurray!" she sang, dancing around the tree. "We're not lost!" Then she turned to Matt. "Where's the rabbit and your cap?"

"Gone, but I don't care. That cap was a pain. It was still stinky with gull poop and seaweed."

Tyrkir pulled out a knife from a pouch at his waist. "I will cut a vine to show Leif what we have discovered. Then we can return later and feast on grapes."

Tyrkir cut a large vine. Then the three of them followed the initialed and numbered trees toward camp. Halfway back, they heard voices. A group of Vikings led by Leif were heading toward them.

"Children! Tyrkir!" shouted Leif, embracing his friend. "We were certain you were devoured by wild beasts. We have been hunting for you since daybreak."

Leif turned and glared at Matt and Emily. "As for you two, you were ordered to stay in camp."

"Do not be angry with the children," said Tyrkir. "I wandered off last night to catch a hare for our meal. The children led me out of the forest and found this!"

Tyrkir held up the grapevine.

"Grapes!" exclaimed Leif. "That is wonderful!"

Leif's face softened as he turned to Matt. "You told us you heard stories about a land full of grapes. Now you have found it." Leif slapped Tyrkir and Matt on the back. "I am happy you are all safe, and that a dragon did not eat you." Leif winked at Emily.

"It couldn't," said Emily, smiling. "There were no dragons in the forest."

"Good," said Leif. "Now, come. Let us prepare a feast. Gunnar has caught many fish. Tyrkir, take three men and bring back as many grapes as you can carry to celebrate our new land.

I will name it Vinland to honour this gift of the vines."

"Hurray! We found Vinland!" said Matt when the Vikings left.

"But Gunnar still has the sled," said Emily. "Where is he anyway?"

"Over there!" said Matt, pointing.

Gunnar was dragging the sled toward the firepit. The sled was loaded with a huge pile of fish. Gunnar let it bounce over the rocks and wood stumps.

Emily cringed at the rough way he was handling the sled. He could break it if he kept loading it with heavy fish and letting it bounce all over the bumpy ground. She had to say something. The sled was their only way home!

She marched over to Gunnar. "That's our sled," she said.

"It is needed for fish," barked Gunnar.

"But it's ours," Emily protested.

"Nothing is yours here."

"When will you give it back?"

"I will not give it back!" boomed Gunnar. "It belongs to all of us now and I am in charge of it."

Emily gulped. What could they do now? Gunnar wanted to keep the sled—forever.

Gunnar began unloading the fish from the sled.

Emily ran over to Matt. "We have to stop him."

"Why don't we help him unload the fish?" Matt whispered. "And when we're done—"

"And he's not looking—" whispered Emily.

"Exactly," said Matt. "It's our only chance."

Matt and Emily ran over to Gunnar. "We can help you unload the fish," they offered, smiling.

"Finally, you are behaving like true Vikings," said Gunnar. For the first time since they met him, a small smile crept up on Gunnar's face.

Emily, Matt, and Gunnar unloaded salmon after salmon on the grass beside the firepit.

When they were almost done, Leif called Gunnar to help bring more wood for the fire. "The children can finish unloading the fish," he said.

Gunnar followed Leif toward the edge of the forest.

"Hurry!" said Matt. "Let's finish before he gets back."

Matt and Emily quickly transferred the last five fish to the grass. Then they grabbed the sled by the rope and ran. As they dashed off, Gunnar strode back with an armful of wood.

"Stop!" he screamed. He dropped the wood and chased after them.

"Quick, Matt! Jump on the sled!" shouted Emily.

Matt shuddered. "The sled is so slimy."

"It's slimy and stinky, too," said Emily. "But we have to get out of here. Fast!"

Emily and Matt hopped on the sled.

"Sled, take us home—please!" said Emily.

Nothing happened.

Gunnar raced toward them. He was only a few steps away from the sled. He reached out, but before he could grab Emily, a hare ran in front of him. Gunnar fell to the ground. The hare scrambled out from under his leg and scampered away.

For a minute, Gunnar lay stunned on the ground. He rubbed his leg, cursing the rabbit. Then he pulled himself up and hobbled toward the sled again.

"Oh no," moaned Emily. "He'll get us!"

"He won't!" said Matt, pointing to the front of the sled. "Look!"

The shimmery gold words were forming at last.

> *You've seen new lands.*
> *You've sailed the sea.*
> *But home's the place*
> *You want to be.*

Matt rubbed the maple leaf three times quickly.

The sled rose. Gunnar tried to yank it down but all he could grab was the air.

The sled soared higher and higher.

Gunnar roared and cursed. But the sled turned and they couldn't see his face or hear his angry words any more.

"Phew," said Emily. "The sled flew us away just in time!"

"I know. Look how high we are already. And there's the ship. It looks like a toy from up here."

"And here comes the cloud. Matt, we're almost home."

They were back!

"Hurray!" said Emily, as the sled landed in the tower room.

Emily slipped off, bent over, and touched the sled. "It isn't slimy or stinky any more. We left the stink and slime back with Gunnar and the Vikings."

"Wasn't it awesome to meet Vikings?" asked Matt, jumping off and stretching.

"It was awesome meeting Leif and Tyrkir," said Emily as they pushed the sled behind the dresser. "But not Gunnar. Anyway, I'm glad we're home and I don't have to eat any more fish."

"I know," said Matt. "I ate more fish in Viking times than in my whole life."

"On our next adventure, I don't want to clean fish or eat them. I want to go somewhere where they bake—blueberry muffins."

"Me, too. But I bet no one anywhere or any time bakes them as well as your mom does," said Matt.

"I know," said Emily, beaming. "My mom's muffins are the best. They're out of this world!"

MORE ABOUT...

After their adventure, Emily and
Matt wanted to know more about
the Vikings. Turn the page for their
favourite facts.

Matt's Top Ten Facts

1. Vikings told sagas, long adventure stories about the history of their people. In the thirteenth century some were written down. We know about Leif and his father, Eric the Red, from the sagas.

2. According to Viking law, every person had a value in money. If you killed someone, you had to pay his relatives.

3. Vikings made skates from bone, skis from wood, and wooden sledges that were pulled by horses.

4. Vikings didn't cook on board ship. They salted fish and bacon to preserve it for a long voyage. They also caught and ate seagulls or fresh fish.

5. The word *berserk* comes from *berserkers*, wild Viking warriors

I'm glad no one asked us to eat seagulls. Yuck!
-E.

who wore wolf skins (heads and all). Sometimes they even attacked their friends.

6. Vikings believed in a heaven called Valhalla. They thought that in Valhalla, you'd live forever, eat big feasts, and practice your battle skills.

7. Vikings saw writing as a special skill. They wrote letters, called runes, which probably came from the Greek and Latin alphabets. Viking runes were carved into stone and wood.

8. Vikings used runes to label and keep records of things they used in their homes.

9. The crew on a *knorr*—and on all Viking ships—had to bail a lot of water. Usually children did the bailing.

10. Viking names tell a story about their life and work. Some names, such as Eric BloodAxe and Thorfinn Skullsplitter, tell us that those Vikings were vicious in battle.

Good thing we didn't meet those guys!

-E.

Emily's Top Ten Facts

1. Viking ships were built to be fast. Long and narrow, they could be rowed by oars or sailed.

2. Vikings usually sailed near shore so they could sleep on land. If they stayed aboard overnight, they curled up in sleeping bags made of sheepskin.

3. To navigate, Viking sailors paid attention to the sun, sea currents, winds, and land and sea creatures. If they had to sail at night, Vikings used the stars to guide them, especially the North Star, Polaris.

4. Here are some words we use today that come from the Norse Viking language: *freckle, skirt, Wednesday,* and *Thursday.*

5. No one knew much about Viking ships until the late 1800s, when ships used to bury Vikings were discovered in pits covered by mounds of dirt.

Dead or alive, Vikings loved to be near ships! —M.

6. Rich Vikings were buried in ships, dressed in their best clothes and with their possessions. Poor Vikings were often buried under part of a ship or in a boat-shaped grave outlined with stones.

7. Most Vikings didn't go on sailing adventures. They stayed home and farmed or raised animals.

8. Viking houses were usually timber, one storey, with a room or two for people, and a spare room for animals. Vikings slept on benches.

9. Vikings usually ate porridge and drank buttermilk for breakfast. They ate using wooden bowls and spoons.

Boy, was I glad to sleep in my own bed after those hard-as-rock benches! —M.

10. Vikings never wore helmets with curled horns. The horn idea came from a nineteenth century opera costume.

WRITE YOUR NAME IN RUNES

I found out how to write my name in runes on the Internet. I just used a search engine and typed in "write your name in runes."

This is matt in runes:

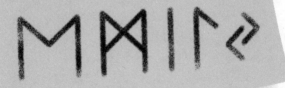

Emily looks like this:

And if there's one thing we've
had enough of it's

ᚠᛁᛊᚾ

The word
fish in runes
looks almost like
the word *fish* in English.
—E

So You Want to Know...

FROM AUTHOR FRIEDA WISHINSKY

When I was researching this book, my friends wanted to know more about Leif Eriksson and the Vikings. I told them that my story is based on historical facts and that Leif and Tyrkir were real people. Other characters such as Gunnar were made up. I also answered these questions:

Who were the Vikings?

The Vikings were Norsemen—people who lived in the Northern part of Europe that is now Norway, Sweden, and Denmark. The term *Viking* means *exploring* in the Norse language. And the Vikings certainly did a lot of that. They sailed to Ireland, England, Flanders, Finland, and to islands in the Baltic Sea. The Vikings sailed quite far in their fast ships.

Many people think that all the Vikings did was plunder and kill the inhabitants of places they invaded. Is that true?

The Vikings could be cruel when they invaded a town or city, but they were also great merchants and explorers. They were always looking for good farmland since some of the lands they had settled, such as Greenland and Iceland, were not fertile.

Where was Leif Eriksson born, and why did he sail to the New World?

Leif was the son of Eric the Red and was born in Iceland in the year 960. He grew up in Greenland. When he heard tales about strange new lands from Bjarni Herjolfsson (who saw the lands but never explored them), Leif bought Bjarni's ship and sailed off to find those lands.

How long did Leif and the Vikings stay in Vinland?

They stayed for just a few years and then returned to Greenland. This was just an exploring expedition. They hadn't planned on staying permanently in Vinland.

Did any other Vikings return to Vinland?

After Leif returned to Greenland, his brother Thorvald and his sister Freydis Eiriksdottir sailed to Vinland with people and livestock to establish a colony. They met and fought with the Native people, whom they called the *Skraeling*, and Thorvald was killed. The Vikings then decided it was too dangerous to stay in this new land.

How do we know the Vikings landed in Vinland?

In 1960, Norwegian explorer and writer Helge Ingstad arrived at a place called L'Anse aux Meadows in Newfoundland after hearing about the remains of an old settlement of turf huts. Helge and his wife, Anne, excavated the area and found numerous Viking artifacts. After careful study of the artifacts, they came to the conclusion that many of the events mentioned in the Viking sagas were true.

Did Helge and Anne find grapevines in Newfoundland?

No. Grapes don't grow in that part of Newfoundland today. But Helge and Anne still believed that what they found was Leif's settlement. As for the absence of grapes, there are a few theories about that. One is that the climate was different in Leif's time, when grapes might have grown. Another theory is that Leif was referring to a different kind of berry, not grapes.

Despite this debate, there is strong evidence that Leif Eriksson and the Vikings were the first Europeans to set foot in North America. The Vikings probably beat Columbus to the New World by almost 500 years.

Send In Your
Top Ten Facts

If you enjoyed this adventure as much as Matt and Emily did, maybe you'd like to collect your own facts about the Vikings, too.

To find out how to send in your favourite facts, visit **www.mapletreepress.com/canadianflyeradventures**. Maple Tree Press will choose the very best facts that are sent in to make *Canadian Flyer Adventures* Readers' Top Ten Lists.

Each reader who sends in a fact that is selected for a Top Ten List will receive a new book in the *Canadian Flyer Adventures* series! (If more than one person sends in the same fact and it is chosen, the first person to submit that fact will be the winner.)

We look forward to hearing from you!

Coming next in the
Canadian Flyer Adventures Series...

Canadian Flyer Adventures
#5

Flying
High!

Turn the page for a sneak peek.

From *Flying High!*

George glanced at his watch. "It's almost three o'clock. When will the Silver Dart fly?"

For the last hour the children had watched as Douglas McCurdy checked and rechecked every part of the airplane.

"What's he waiting for?" asked Matt.

A few minutes later they knew. A horse-drawn sleigh drove up, and out climbed Alexander Graham Bell dressed in a large furry coat. He marched over to McCurdy and put his arm around the young flyer. "Are you ready?"

Douglas nodded and pulled his stocking cap tight over his ears. He stepped into the airplane, sat down, and signaled. Eight men hurried over to hold the airplane steady.

The crowd backed off as another man ran over and spun the propeller. The Dart's engine belched out a cloud of smoke and snow.

"I hope Mr. McCurdy knows what he's doing," said George. "It looks scary to go up in that airplane. He could fall out."

George, Matt, Emily, and Ruby stared as Douglas McCurdy gave another signal. The men holding the airplane let go and hurried out of the way.

The Dart zoomed down the ice. It moved faster and faster. But then, instead of lifting off the ground, it stopped.

The crowd gasped. Douglas hopped out and scurried to the side of the airplane.

A few people in the crowd laughed. Mr. McNeil said, "I told you that contraption wouldn't fly."

But some people called out words of support.

"Give the lad another chance!"

McCurdy ignored all the comments. He inspected the airplane carefully and fiddled with the gas pump. Then he asked the men to pull the airplane back to its starting position.

The crowd fell silent again. Everybody held their breath. Would the Dart fly this time or would it fail again?

The children's eyes were glued to the airplane as the propeller spun again....

The *Canadian Flyer Adventures* Series

#1 Beware, Pirates!
#2 Danger, Dinosaurs!
#3 Crazy for Gold
#4 Yikes, Vikings!

Upcoming Book

Look out for the next book that will take
Emily and Matt on a new adventure.

#5 Flying High!

And more to come!

About the Author

Frieda Wishinsky, a former teacher, is an award-winning picture- and chapter-book author, who has written many beloved and bestselling books for children. Frieda enjoys using humour and history in her work, while exploring new ways to tell a story. Her books have earned much critical praise, including a nomination for a Governor General's Award in 1999. In addition to the books in the *Canadian Flyer Adventures* series, Frieda has published *What's the Matter with Albert?*, *A Quest in Time*, and *Manya's Dream* with Maple Tree Press. Frieda lives in Toronto.

About the Illustrator

Gordon Dean Griffiths realized his love for drawing very early in life. At the age of 12, halfway through a comic book, Dean decided that he wanted to become a comic book artist and spent every spare minute of the next few years perfecting his art. In 1995 Dean illustrated his first children's book, *The Patchwork House*, written by Sally Fitz-Gibbon. Since then he has happily illustrated over a dozen other books for young people and is currently working on several more, including the *Canadian Flyer Adventures* series. Dean lives in Duncan, B.C.